This book belongs to:

....

....

....

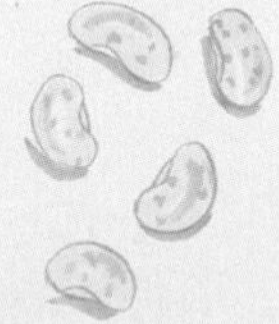
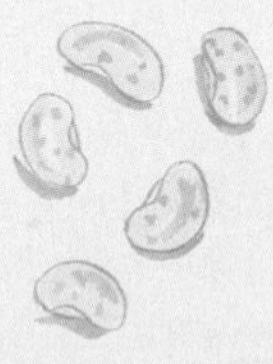
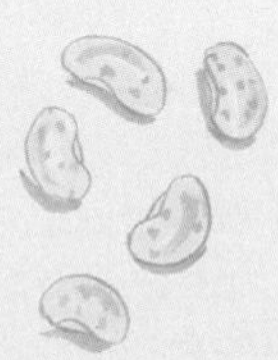
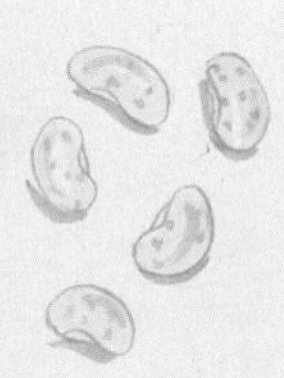

Retold by Gaby Goldsack
Illustrated by Kim Blundell
Designed by Jester Designs

Language consultant: Betty Root

ISBN 1-40545-558-6

This is a Parragon Publishing Book
This edition published in 2005

Parragon Publishing
Queen Street House
4 Queen Street
Bath BA1 1HE, UK

Printed in India

p

Jack and the Beanstalk

Helping your Child Read

Learning to read is an exciting challenge for most children. From a very early age, sharing storybooks with children, talking about the pictures, and guessing what might happen next are all very important parts of the reading experience.

Sharing reading

Set aside a regular quiet time to share reading with younger children, or to be on hand to encourage older children as they develop into independent readers.

First Readers are intended to encourage and support the early stages of learning to read. They present much-loved tales that children will happily listen to again and again. Familiarity helps children identify some of the words and phrases.

When you feel that your child is ready to move on a little, encourage him or her to join in so that you read the story aloud together. Always pause to talk about the pictures. The easy-to-read speech bubbles in **First Readers** provide an excellent 'joining-in' activity. The bright, clear illustrations and matching text will help children understand the story.

Building confidence

In time, children will want to read *to* you. When this happens, be patient and give continual praise. They may not read all the words correctly, but children's substitutions are often very good guesses.

The repetition in each book is particularly helpful for building confidence. If your child cannot read a particular word, go back to the beginning of the sentence and read it together so the meaning is not lost. Most important, do not continue if your child is tired or just needs a break.

Reading alone

The next step is to ask your child to read alone. Try to be on hand to give help and support. Remember to give lots of encouragement and praise.

Along with other simple stories, **First Readers** will ensure that children will find reading an enjoyable and rewarding experience.

Jack, sell the cow.

Once upon a time a boy named Jack lived with his mother.

Jack and his mother were very poor. All they had was an old cow.

One day, Jack's mother said, "We must sell the cow."
"I'll take her to market," said Jack.

Jack went to market.

Along the way he met an old man.

"I'll give you five magic beans for the cow," said the old man.

"Five beans!" said Jack.
"That's not much."
"But these are magic beans,"
said the old man.
So Jack took the beans and the
old man took the cow.

Jack went home.

He was very pleased.

He gave his mother the five beans.

She was not pleased.

"Magic beans!" she cried. "They are no good!" And she threw them out of the window.

She sent Jack to bed without any supper.

In the morning, Jack woke up.
He looked out of his window.
The beans had grown in the night.

They had grown into
a giant beanstalk.
It went up and up
into the clouds.

Jack began to climb
the beanstalk.

He climbed up and up.

He climbed above the clouds.

At last he reached the top.

At the top of the beanstalk was
a giant castle.

Jack went into the giant castle.
He found a giant kitchen.
There was plenty of food to eat.
Suddenly Jack heard a gruff voice.

"Fee-fi-fo-fum!" roared the voice.

Jack hid in a closet.

He peeped out.

A giant came into the kitchen.

The giant sat at the table.

He had a hen.

"Hen, lay an egg," said the giant.

The hen clucked and laid a golden egg!

The giant ate a giant dinner.

Then he went to sleep.

Jack crept out of the closet.

He crept to the table.

He took the hen.

The hen clucked and the giant woke up!

The giant saw Jack.

"Fee-fi-fo-fum!" he roared.

Jack ran and ran.
He climbed down
and down the
beanstalk.

The giant was not far behind.
Jack reached the bottom.

He got an ax and chopped down the beanstalk.

The giant came crashing down.

And that was the end of the giant.

Jack's mother was pleased because the hen laid golden eggs.
Jack and his mother were never poor again.

Golden eggs!
Hen, lay an egg!

Read and Say

How many of these words can you say? The pictures will help you. Look back in your book and see if you can find the words in the story.

castle

old man

ax

food

giant

window